BIO

1595

W9-DGB-462

HERO on HORSEBACK

Important Dates
in the
Life of Casimir Pulaski

1747	Born March 4 in Poland
1752-1764	Attended school in Winiary and Warsaw, Poland
1767	Joined Knights of the Holy Cross Army
1767-1772	Fought for Poland against Russia
1774	Imprisoned in France
1777	Sailed for America in May
1777	Appointed Chief of American Cavalry in September
1779	Died October 11 of wounds suffered in battle

HERO on HORSEBACK
The Story of Casimir Pulaski

By David R. Collins
Illustrated by Larry Nolte

PELICAN PUBLISHING COMPANY

*The word "Pelican" and the depiction of a pelican are trademarks
of Pelican Publishing Company, Inc., and are registered
in the U.S. Patent and Trademark Office.*

Library of Congress Cataloging-in-Publication Data

Collins, David R.
      Hero on horseback : the story of Casimir Pulaski / by David R.
      Collins ; illustrated by Larry Nolte.
            p.   cm.
      Summary: Presents the life of the American Revolutionary War hero,
from his childhood in Poland to his role in developing a cavalry
unit for the American patriots and his death in battle.
      ISBN 1-56554-266-5 (alk. paper)
      1. Pulaski, Kazimierz, 1747-1779—Juvenile literature.
2. Generals—United States—Biography—Juvenile literature.
3. Generals—Poland—Biography—Juvenile literature. 4. United
States. Army—Biography—Juvenile literature. 5. United States—
History—Revolution, 1775-1783—Biography—Juvenile literature.
[1. Pulaski, Casimir, 1747-1779. 2. Generals. 3. United States—
History—Revolution, 1775-1783.] I. Nolte, Larry, ill.
II. Title.
E207.P8C65 1997
973.3'46—dc21   96-54009
                                                                                    CIP
                                                                                     AC

Printed in Hong Kong

Published by Pelican Publishing Company, Inc.
1101 Monroe Street, Gretna, LA 70053

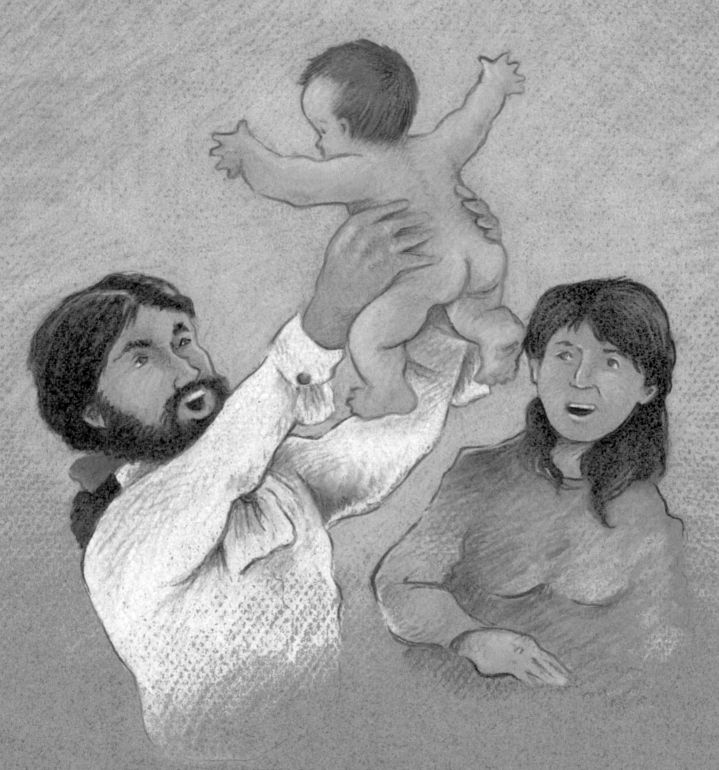

HERO on HORSEBACK
The Story of Casimir Pulaski

Young Casimir Pulaski was a wiggler. People said he wiggled
from the moment he was born. That was on March 4, 1747.

Young Casimir wiggled as he sat on his father's lap. Joseph Pulaski was a rich lawyer in Poland. Every day people came to talk to Casimir's father.

Casimir wiggled when he sat next to his mother. Marianne Pulaski read to her son every day. She played the piano for him too.

"You are a child of God, a son of Poland, and a Pulaski." Young Casimir heard those words often. The boy knew that much was expected of him.

Casimir tried hard in school. The work did not come easy for him. He wiggled a lot on his wooden school bench.

But he never wiggled when he rode horseback. Casimir was a quick learner in the saddle. Michael, the stableman, taught him. Casimir learned how to mount and dismount. He learned how to start and stop. He learned how to circle and jump.

Casimir and his friends played war games on horseback. They carved wooden lances and speared apples on fence posts. They learned how to shoot muskets as they rode. "I hope war will always be just a game for you," Casimir's father would say.

In 1767 Russian soldiers crossed over into Poland. The Russians wanted Poland's rich farmlands. The king of Poland did nothing about it.

"We must be a free people!" Joseph Pulaski said. But most Polish people went about their business. More Russian soldiers marched into Poland.

Joseph Pulaski raised an army. He called his soldiers the Knights of the Holy Cross. "We will fight to keep this country free!" the brave lawyer said.

Twenty-year-old Casimir Pulaski joined his father's army. He showed men how to ride and shoot. "No one rides and shoots as well as young Pulaski," they all said.

Casimir got plenty of chances to show his skills. He led his soldiers all over Poland. They fought the Russians on hillsides and fields. They fought the Russians in the forests and forts. "Casimir Pulaski is a brave soldier," people said.

One night the Russians played a dirty trick. They kidnapped the king of Poland. Then the Russians blamed it on Casimir Pulaski! The king of Poland could not name his kidnappers. It was too dark for him to see. Still the Russians said it was Casimir. Some of the people wondered.

More and more Russian soldiers came into Poland. Casimir fought as hard as he could. Often he was outnumbered. Yet he won many battles.

Casimir's father was arrested and died in a prison. Casimir's brother was killed in battle. Casimir was forced to flee his own country.

Casimir went from one country to another. He tried to raise money so he could start a new army. No one would help.

Casimir ran out of money in France. The police arrested him for not paying his debts. They threw Casimir in prison.

While he was in prison, Casimir heard about another war. British soldiers were fighting American soldiers across the sea. It was just like the Russians against the Polish.

When he got out of prison, Casimir went to see Benjamin Franklin. Franklin was the American ambassador to France. "I want to help the Americans fight the British," said Casimir.

"But America is not your country," said Franklin. "I know," answered Casimir. "I want to fight for freedom, not just a country."

Benjamin Franklin smiled. "I will send you to George Washington in America. "I think he can use you."

Casimir Pulaski sailed for America in May of 1777. When he arrived, he went to see George Washington. General Washington was the leader of the American soldiers.

Casimir shared his thoughts about fighting wars. He was sure soldiers on horseback could help the Americans. Washington agreed.

Casimir went right to work. He went around gathering men.
Soon the young man from Poland was training soldiers again.

Casimir demanded that his soldiers be ready for battle. He
drilled them hard in shooting and riding. He developed stronger
lances with steel tips. He designed special uniforms so his men
would be recognized.

Soon Casimir led his cavalry into battle. They made quick surprise attacks. They caught the British soldiers off guard.

In the darkness of night Casimir's cavalry attacked. In the thickness of forests and on open fields they attacked. "Charge!" was a word Casimir and his men knew well. They swooped down on the enemy soldiers.

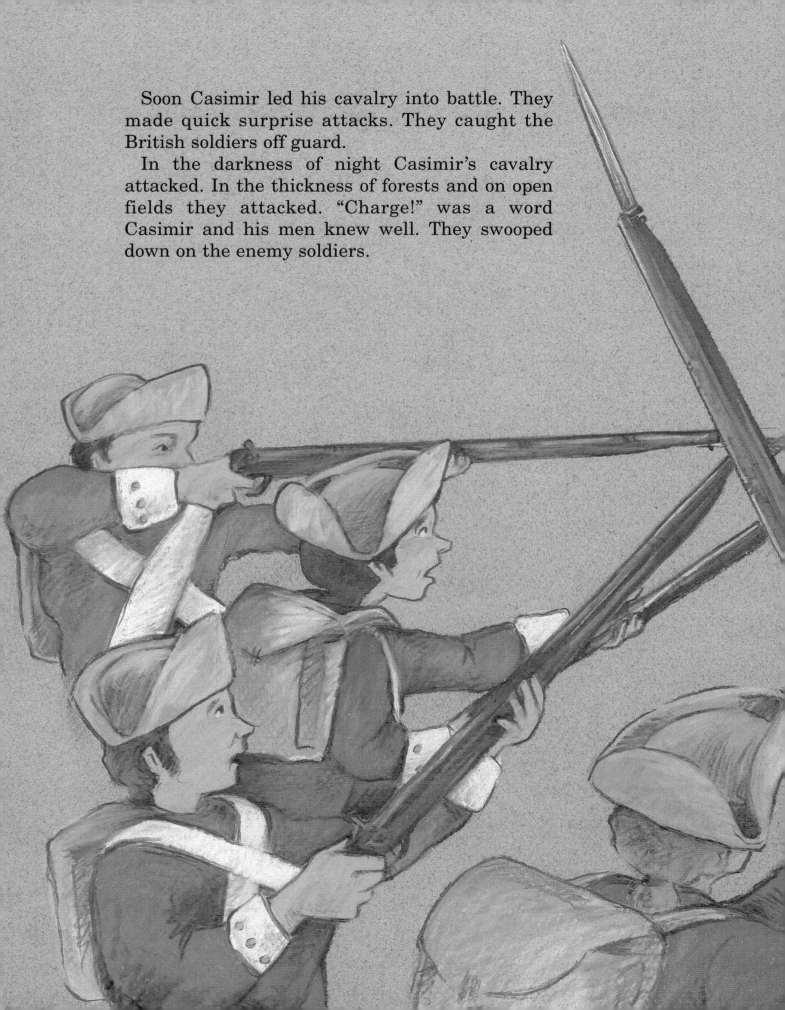

Casimir was made a general of the American army. General Washington was glad Pulaski had joined the fight. The soldier from Poland helped win many battles.

But not everyone liked the way Casimir acted. He took supplies and horses from American farmers. "I need them for my soldiers," he said.

Others complained that he was from another country. "He doesn't even speak our language," some grumbled. Casimir pretended not to hear the complaints. He had more important work to do.

The Americans won more and more battles. Casimir's cavalry captured more British soldiers and supplies. They chased British soldiers into the South.

By the fall of 1779, the Americans were winning the war. Casimir Pulaski led his soldiers to Savannah, Georgia. They approached a British camp. "Charge!" Casimir called out.

Casimir's cavalry thundered forward. Bullets shot out everywhere. Two of those bullets hit Casimir.

Casimir's soldiers took him to a nearby ship. The doctors operated, but it was too late. Casimir Pulaski died on October 14, 1779. He was thirty-two years old.

"Casimir Pulaski was a true hero," said General George Washington. "He did not give his life for his country. He gave his life for freedom."